Making Me Believe
By Kirsten Osbourne

Chapter 1

Rose shoved the last load of her laundry into the dryer and climbed onto the counter of the small apartment laundromat. She picked up her novel and opened to the page she'd left off on. Another Friday night, another three loads of laundry. Rose always did her laundry on Friday nights. She didn't have to work the next day, and no one else was ever there to fight her for the washers and dryers. It was a great situation for her.

She was halfway through her chapter when she heard the door open. She hadn't seen anyone in there for the past three weeks, so she immediately looked up to see who else could have such a sad lack of a social life that they would be doing laundry on a Friday night.

Her eyes opened wide as she stared at the gorgeous man who'd just walked in. He must have been at least six foot three with broad shoulders. Rose grinned to herself as she watched him over the top of her book. He had black hair, and it looked like brown eyes, but it was hard to tell from here. He was trim and muscular. Rose tried not to drool.

He was carrying two huge black trash bags that were apparently full of laundry. He was either married with six kids and doing the laundry for the whole family, or he had waited way too long to do his laundry. Rose lifted her eyes again to check out his left hand, but there was no ring on his finger. He must have not done laundry in forever.

He opened the garbage bags and started to dump all of the laundry into one washer, not paying any attention to what he was mixing together. Rose cringed and put her book down.

"You can't wash all that without sorting it," she told him. "Let me help you."

He shrugged, "I always do. It takes longer if I sort it."

"Are you late for something? Most people who do laundry on a Friday night are sadly lacking in the social life department," she said. "So unless you have a hot date that starts sometime after midnight, then you may as well do it right."

"No, I'm not in a hurry. I just have to work in the morning, and don't want to be at this all night," he said. He shrugged. If she wanted to help him sort his laundry, he was game. There were worse ways to spend an evening that with a pretty girl in a laundromat. Of course, there were much better ways to spend an evening as well!

"It'll only take an extra five minutes if we work together. Put some money into five washing machines and I'll start sorting," she said. She immediately started pulling the clothes he'd packed into the first washer out and spreading them across the first four washers. She put jeans in the first one, colors in the second, whites in the third and towels in the fourth. If he was anything like her, they'd put more colors in the fifth, but whatever it was that needed to go in there, she knew they'd need at least five washers. They ended up needing eight.

Once they had everything sorted, and the machines going, she settled back down onto the counter with her book. He walked over and hoisted himself up next to her, taking her book from her hands. "Hey this is sci-fi! I figured you for a romance reader."

She shrugged. "I do read romance. It's my secret pleasure. I only read sci-fi in public."

He laughed. "I see. I think I do at least." He looked down at her, liking the way she looked. She was wearing a pair of faded warm ups and a t-shirt, which was a smart choice for laundry on a March night in North Texas. Her long blond hair was pulled back into a ponytail. Her eyes looked green, but it was hard to tell from this angle. "Do you always do your laundry on Friday nights?"

"Of course, I do," she grinned. "I have no life!"

"Okie dokie. I can understand that. I don't really have a life either, but I never do my laundry until it threatens to swallow my apartment whole. I hate laundry," he said.

"I do too. That's why I do it every Friday night like clockwork. It never piles up and I never have to do eight loads in one night. You do realize we just started eight loads of laundry for you, right?"

"Don't remind me. I don't even want to think about it," he told her. "Thanks for the help, by the way. I'm sure I'll be thrilled when my socks stay white and don't turn pink from my red t-shirts."

"No problem. I had nothing better to do while I sit here and wait for my clothes to dry," she said.

"I'm Alex," he said holding his hand out to her to shake.

She took his hand in hers. "I'm Rose. Please don't quote *Romeo and Juliet* to me."

He looked puzzled. "Why would I quote *Romeo and Juliet*? Oh! I get it. That whole "a rose by any other name" or something like that."

"Yes and every literate male I meet quotes that to me. You seem literate, but don't do it. It gets old fast."

He laughed, "I can understand that. No one ever quotes Shakespeare to me. Does that mean that there's something wrong with me?" He had his head tilted to the side as if he was genuinely worried about the fact.

"Nope. It just means your parents didn't name you after a flower." Rose sighed heavily. She'd always hated her name. She'd thought about going by her middle name, but that was Lily, which was just as bad. Her mother had a gardening obsession.

"I have to say, I'm really glad they didn't."

She grinned, "I don't know. It could have been a good conversation starter. Do you mind if I call you Tulip?" He loved the impish grin on her face as if she was daring him to agree to her suggestion.

"How about I just come up with a conversation starter instead?" He sat thinking for a moment. "Okay, I got it. Are you ready?" His brown eyes twinkled down at her as he asked.

She tried to suppress a giggle. He was crazy, but in a fun way. "Wait, let me brace myself." She grabbed onto the counter tightly. "Okay, I'm ready." Rose couldn't believe a total stranger could make laundry night fun.

"Hi, my name is Alex, and I'm making a bid for world domination. Would you be my follower?" he asked.

Rose threw back her head and laughed. "That's a good one. I don't think anyone would ever talk to you twice, but it's a good conversation starter!" It sounded like something she might say herself.

Alex looked at the pretty little girl sitting next to him on the counter, trying to figure out why she had no social life. She was sweet, had a sense of humor, and was cute as a button. He loved the way she laughed. So many women seemed afraid to laugh heartily. Why was she in a laundromat on a Friday night?

He grinned down at her. "How about this one? What's a pretty girl like you doing in a place like this on a Friday night?"

"I already told you that, Alex. Try to pay attention. I hate laundry so try to finish it first thing on the weekend, and I have no life."

He shook his head slowly. "That's not going to cut it. There's got to be a reason you have no life. You're fun, pretty, and outgoing. Why do you have no life? And did you just tell me to try to pay attention?" She was not like others girls; that was for sure.

She shrugged. "I don't put out. I'm very vocal about it too. I think that sex should only take place within the confines of marriage. Call me old-fashioned. Call me boring and ridiculous. I don't care."

He nodded slowly. "That would explain it. Are you a religious nut, or just a girl with standards?"

She smiled at him. "I'm a girl with standards. I think that if a guy loves me enough to do me, he needs to love me enough to buy me a ring, and walk down the aisle. If not, there are lots of girls who put out in every bar in town. He can go find one of them."

He nodded again. "I can respect that. So you're holding out for a ring, because there's no reason to buy the cow if you can get the milk for free?"

"There's no point in locking the barn door after the horse is out," she replied seriously.

"Guys rent used furniture, but they only buy new," he responded.

She laughed. "I haven't heard that one before. I love it!" She had always loved idioms, and was pleased to add another to her repertoire.

One of the dryers buzzed and she jumped down off the counter. "You can't be finished," he complained. "I need you to stay and talk to me!" He wasn't ready to let her go yet. He had to get to know her better. Maybe he could talk her into giving him her number before she left. He didn't care if she didn't put out. She was fun to be around.

"I'm probably not. They usually take two cycles to finish." She glanced at him. "You should bring a book so you don't get bored."

"Why? I'd rather talk to you," he responded.

"So you're going to start joining me for Friday night laundry," she asked with a grin. She didn't expect him to do it, but it would be great if she had a laundry buddy. Of course, the real reason she wanted him to do laundry with her was so she could get to know him better.

He shuddered. "Not if I can avoid it!" he said. "Although, it's a whole lot more fun with you here." He winked at her.

"Thanks. I think." She restarted her three dryers again, and walked back over to him and her book. She put her bookmark in the book and closed it. There was no point in even trying to read when she was entertained far better by the man sitting next to her.

"So I get you for a little bit longer?" he asked.

She just laughed at that. "I guess so. Probably another thirty minutes, and then I'll fold my laundry, and head on back to my lonely apartment. I need to get a goldfish. A goldfish would keep me company."

"Dogs are better," he responded quickly.

"I'm away fourteen hours a day half the time. That wouldn't be fair to a dog. No, it'll have to be a goldfish." She definitely would have preferred a dog, though.

"Too bad you don't put out," he said jokingly, "I'm sure you'd never be lonely again."

"I'm sure," she laughed.

"Do you clean your bathrooms on Saturday nights?" he asked.

"Nah, I usually get that done on Saturday mornings. Every Saturday night, I make a date with my TV, and catch up on watching everything that I DVRed the week before."

"You really are a wild woman!" he said.

"I know. I can barely stand the crazy life I lead. Do you know that last week, when I mopped my kitchen, I turned the music up loud, and actually danced with the mop? It was just scandalous!" She said it with an air of secrecy, like she was almost afraid to admit she'd done something like that.

"That sounds scandalous!" he said with a shocked look on his face. "I'm so glad no one was there to see that! You could have been arrested for indecent behavior!"

"I know. I'm really ashamed of myself," she said with her head down.

"How about doing something more scandalous tomorrow night, and going out to dinner with me?" He hadn't meant to ask so abruptly, but he had to make sure he'd see her again soon.

She laughed. "Because you're looking for a girl who isn't going to put out, I'm sure. All men are." She didn't believe that he was actually asking her out. Most men were scared off as soon as she said she didn't put out before marriage.

"What I'm looking for is a girl with a sense of humor, who hasn't slept with every man she's met, who wants to have some fun with me," he said seriously. "How about it?" He tried to keep the desperation from his voice as he asked. He really did want to go out with her. She was special.

She shrugged. "Okay. I can do that." She was more than willing to spend time with this great guy. She just hoped he realized she was serious about not having sex before marriage.

They got up, and she helped him transfer his laundry into dryers. "Great. I'll pick you up at six."

"Okay," she said.

He pulled out his cell phone and input the number she gave him. "Just in case I'm going to be late, I'll give you a call."

They got back onto the counter where they'd been sitting. "You said you had to work in the morning," she said. "What do you do?"

"Aren't you supposed to ask me that before you agree to go out with me? I mean, what if I'm a trash collector?" he asked.

"I don't really care what you do. I'll go out with you anyway. I wouldn't date someone on the merit of his occupation. I'm just curious."

"I'm an architect, but I own my own construction firm, and with all the rain we've had, we're behind on a project. I need to go check it out tomorrow, and see how everything is going. The client wants a projected date when we'll be finished."

"That sounds like it could be exciting," she told him. "What kind of project is it?"

"Some crazy rich guy wanted me to custom design a home for him. He's going to be moving up to Westlake," he said naming a high dollar community north of Ft. Worth. "This place has it all. Indoor pool and tennis court, family kitchen and catering kitchen had to be separate. It's crazy what all he wanted, but he was willing to pay well, so we did it. I'm hoping to have the whole project done by the end of next month," he told her.

"Wow. I hope he has a family to live in it with him," she said.

"He's a newlywed, and they're hoping to have a big family. They both come from money, and he makes good money in his daddy's company, so they're getting exactly what they want," he said. "Some people have more money than brains, and this couple is a good example of that."

"It sounds like it," she responded. "I joke about wanting a place like that, but I couldn't afford the maid that I'd want to go with it. I can't imagine cleaning that kind of space."

"People don't really need that kind of space, unless they have fifteen or sixteen kids." He stretched, starting to find sitting on the counter uncomfortable. "What do you do?"

She sighed heavily. "I work in a cube talking on the phone all day," she replied. "I talk to rich people about their money." She hated her job. She knew it came out in her voice, but she just couldn't stop it.

"That sounds horrible," he said without thinking.

She wrinkled her nose. "It really is. I want to own a little used bookstore and sit behind the desk and talk to people about good books all day long. I hate what I do." She didn't usually talk to people about her dream of owning a bookstore, but she found herself wanting to tell him every detail of her life.

"Do you work for a bank?"

"Even worse," she said. "I work for a brokerage firm. It pays well, and I'm good at it, but I hate it. I'm saving, though, and someday soon, I'll have the money to start my little bookstore."

"Good for you. I hope you have it soon. I can't imagine you with one of those little antenna things on your head talking on the phone all day," he said. "I can see you in a bookstore, though. You'd bring people back with your pleasant chatter."

"That's exactly what it feels like too. It makes my ear itch," she sighed. "I'm always working as many hours as I can get so that I can save up enough for the bookstore. I've been out of college for two years now, and I figure I have about half of what I'll need."

"You could give up on your bookstore and become my campaign manager instead," he told her.

"Campaign manager?" Was he running for office? What was she missing?

"I'm taking over the world. Did you already forget?" he asked.

All of the dryers started buzzing, and they got down. He restarted his, and she took her clothes out and folded them neatly, putting them on hangers, and resting them in the laundry baskets she'd brought with her.

He watched her work, and finally said, "I need to get some of those things."

"What things?" she asked.

He pointed at the basket. "Those things. Then my dirty laundry would stay contained and not threaten my apartment the way it usually does." He joked about it, but he really wasn't exaggerating. His apartment was downright scary to walk into.

She looked up at him. "I like you. You scare me, but I like you." She picked up the first basket and started toward the door to the laundry room. "Watch my other basket for me. I wouldn't want the stampeding herds of people who come here to do laundry on Friday nights to steal my clothes."

He picked up her other basket. "I'll just carry it for you. That way I'll know where you live, and won't have to hunt up your apartment tomorrow night." He wanted to see her space as well. He expected it to be neat as a pin, but wanted to know. He wanted to know everything about her.

"Okay," she agreed. She wasn't going to argue with that. She hated walking through the parking lot alone after dark anyway.

He followed her across the wide parking lot and down a level to her apartment. She unlocked the door, and he followed her in, putting the basket on her kitchen table for her.

"Is it always this neat?" he asked. He'd expected it, but he was shocked by just how neat it was. There wasn't a single dirty dish in the sink.

"Well, I'm the only one who lives here. I'm capable of picking up after myself, so it just doesn't get dirty," she said.

"Remind me to never show you my apartment," he told her. "I think you'd be pretty disgusted."

"Typical male?" she asked. He struck her as someone who could be very organized and take care of things well, but he had to care first. She doubted he cared about how his apartment looked.

"Yeah, I'm afraid so. My sister used to try to hire cleaning girls for me, but they'd take one step inside the door and run away screaming. It was sad. She stopped trying," he said.

She rolled her eyes at him. "Go back and babysit your laundry," she said. "I'll see you tomorrow night." He was halfway to the door, when she stopped him, "What should I wear? Jeans okay?"

"Yeah, jeans are fine. We'll go somewhere casual."

"Sounds good," she said as she shut the door behind him.

Chapter 2

Rose got up early to get done with her chores the following morning. She didn't really have anything that she wanted to wear on a date. Since she'd graduated from college two years before, she hadn't been willing to spend any more money than absolutely necessary. Work clothes were a necessity. Workout clothes were a necessity. Workout clothes could be worn for laundry and errands. Why did she need nice jeans?

Tonight, she needed a nice pair of jeans. She needed a pretty blouse. She may even need some cowboy boots. She'd moved to North Texas when she was sixteen, and had gone to college in Arlington, where she still lived. Her parents had long since moved back to Illinois where she'd grown up, but she'd stayed for college, and had found a job in nearby Fort Worth when she'd graduated.

Every extra dime had gone straight into savings. Maybe it was time she lightened up and lived a little. She could spend a little bit of that savings. Rose spent the afternoon wandering around the mall, looking for just the right clothes. She found a pair of jeans that fit her body snugly, but not so tightly that she couldn't breathe easily. She hated jeans that were that tight, and couldn't understand why any woman would wear them that way.

They fit so well that she bought two pairs. You never knew when you'd need jeans.

She found a buy two get one free sale on blouses at a favorite store of hers. She'd bought some blouses from there while she was in college, but they were long since in ruins. She wasn't into shopping, and tended to wear her clothes until they were stained or falling apart. She bought three blouses and headed out.

She went to a small western store and found a pair of pink cowboy boots. She'd never been big into cowboy boots, but she did love pink ones. She'd debated buying a pair on and off during her eight years in Texas.

She arrived home around 4:30 and started to get ready for her date. She had dated very little over the years, which was mainly due to her outspokenness. She had given every man who had looked at her twice her opinions about sex before marriage, and most had either been looking only for sex, or had just not been willing to date someone who was as outspoken as she was. Either way, she was happy to get them out of the way. She wasn't in any kind of hurry to get married. If the right guy proposed, then sure. Otherwise, she was young and had a goal.

She was ready at 5:45 and grabbed her nook which contained the romance novel that she was currently engrossed in. She curled up on the couch and read until she heard a knock. She shut off her nook and set it on the coffee table. She quickly went to the door and opened it. She'd chosen to wear jeans, a soft pink button up blouse, and her new cowboy boots.

Alex stood there in a pair of jeans, a western shirt, and a pair of cowboy boots. He grinned at her. "You look great." His made no effort to hide theway his eyes slid over her from head to toe.

Rose almost felt as if his hand had stroked up her body. She was amazed at just how sexually aware she was of this man. She'd never met anyone who made her feel this way. "Thanks. You look pretty good yourself," she told him.

He handed her a bouquet of carnations, and she buried her nose in them, and then went to the kitchen to put them in water. "I love them! Thank you. Come on in while I find something to put these in." She didn't have a vase, so she used a water glass.

He followed her to the kitchen and watched her, leaning lazily against the counter. "I thought we'd go out to a steak place I know. They have dancing and a good Country band most nights," he said. "It's not a bar, but they do serve alcohol. I hope that's all right."

"Sounds great! I love to dance," she said. "I'm not much of a drinker, but I don't have a problem if you want a drink or two."

"I don't drink," he said. He didn't elaborate, but she had a feeling there was a story in there somewhere.

"Let me get my jacket, and I'll be ready to go," she told him. She grabbed her jacket off the chair where she'd laid it earlier, and slipped it on. He held the door for her and even took her key to lock it.

"I do know how to lock my own door, you know," she said. She didn't mind that he was doing it for her, but she felt she needed to make at least a token protest.

"I know. My mama always taught me that a gentleman locked and unlocked doors for his date. So that's what I do," he explained.

"That works. Tell me about your mama," she said. She'd always thought that you could tell a lot about a man by how he felt about his mother.

He led her to a dark blue pick-up truck and opened the passenger door for her. "Well, let's see." He walked around the truck and got in beside her.

"She was a great mom. She was a teacher when she and Dad were first married, but decided to stay home to raise us. She always had a snack ready when we got home from school. Now that Dad is retired, they're travelling around North America in an RV."

"Sounds like fun to me! Did you grow up here in Arlington?" she asked.

"Yep. I lived in the same house from the day I was born until I graduated from college."

"Wow. That must have been great. We moved around quite a bit because my dad was a manager for a retail chain. They'd move us to new areas to open new stores, and then move us again once it was up and running," she said. "My parents have moved back to Illinois, and Dad said he's not moving again."

"So that Yankee accent I hear is Illinois? I was wondering."

Rose sighed. "After eight years, you can still hear the accent?" When she first moved to Texas, she didn't think that the Mid-Western states had accents. Now when she went back to visit, she would almost cringe at the strong nasal voices.

"Once a Yankee, always a Yankee," he teased. "Did you have to show them your green card when you started your job?"

"You're one of those, are you?" she asked, referring to native Texans who tended to think that everyone from any other state was a foreigner.

"Yes, ma'am, I'm proud of it too!" he grinned.

She laughed. Looking out the window she realized they were headed north on highway 360 and had left Arlington behind. "Where are we going? I figured you'd take me somewhere in Arlington."

"Nahh. I found this great little place up in Grapevine. I figured I'd take you there. I get more time in your company that way," he said.

"Okay," she answered. "You said your mom stayed home with 'us'. How many brothers and sisters do you have?"

"It's just me and my kid sister, Sarah. She's married and has a little boy. They live here in Arlington. How 'bout you? Any brothers or sisters?"

"I'm an only. My mom always wanted more, but it just didn't happen." She knew her mother had been disappointed in only having one child, and she'd really been torn up when Rose had decided to stay in Texas when they moved back home. They remained close, though.

"So were you a typical spoiled only?" he asked.

"I don't think so. I mean, my parents made sure I knew that I was the center of their world, but I didn't get everything I wanted whenever I wanted it. They expected me to work hard and get good grades. I had to get summer jobs in high school, and they expected me to get a scholarship to pay as much of my way through college as I could."

"Sounds like they raised you right," he said with a grin. "That's the kind of parent I plan to be someday."

"I'm so glad you approve," she said sarcastically. She did note that he wanted children. That was definitely a point in his favor.

He laughed and said, "You should be! I'm the most important man in this truck!"

"You sure are!" She grinned. "How did work go today?"

"It was good. I think we should be done within the next couple of weeks, and that thrilled the client. I'm ready to move on to other projects," he said.

"What do you have in the works?" she asked.

"Just some more houses. I think that's going to be my niche. Custom homes. I have no desire to design the cookie cutter homes that you find in every neighborhood."

"How long have you had your own business?" she asked.

"My dad was an architect. When I graduated, I worked with him for a couple of years, and then he retired, and I took it over. It's been mine for about four years now. Some of the guys who have been there forever still think of me as the boss's kid."

"Does that make it tough?" she asked. She couldn't imagine having to constantly live in her father's shadow.

He shrugged. "I guess it did at first, but now it's no big deal. They always do what I say, and that's what matters when you get right down to it." He pulled the truck into the parking lot of a small restaurant.

He ran around the truck to open her door for her, taking her hand and helping her down. "Those manners your mama taught you seem to have stuck," she said.

"They better have! She'd take after me with a wooden spoon if they hadn't," he said with a grin.

"Are you afraid of your mama?" she asked with a laugh.

"Every smart southern man is afraid of his mama. You never outgrow having to listen to her. Never," he said seriously.

He opened the door for her, and they went into the restaurant. He'd made reservations and they were led to a corner booth. He waited until she slid into one side, and then he slid into the other.

"I'm glad you're not one of those who thinks we need to sit on one side together. That always looks weird to me," she said.

"I think so too," he told her quietly. "Besides, I want to be able to watch your pretty face as we talk."

She looked down at her menu, a little flustered by the compliment. "What's good here?"

"The steak is great. I haven't bothered to try anything else, because it's a steak place, and it's Texas. If you get the chicken, you're liable to be run out of town," he told her.

"I think I'll have a steak," she said with a laugh.

"I think that's a fabulous choice," he told her with a wink.

The waiter was there then asking for their drink orders. "I'll just have water," she told him. "No lemon, please."

Alex asked for a sweet tea, and as the waiter walked away he asked, "What is it with always putting lemon in people's water anyway? I mean, if you want lemonade, you order lemonade. Water should be just that. Water."

"No kidding! That's a major pet peeve of mine. I hate lemon in my water. I don't understand why people want it, or why restaurants expect everyone to like it that way," she sighed. "I like water. Plain boring old water."

He reached out and took her hand in his. He slowly rubbed his thumb over her palm. "I assume hand holding before marriage is okay?"

"I can make an exception, just this once," she returned with a smile. She felt a tingle shoot through her. She knew most girls thought handholding was boring, but she'd done so little of it, that it was actually exciting for her.

The waiter came back with their drinks, and they ordered their meals. As soon as the waiter walked off, he stood and pulled her to her feet. "Dance with me, Rose."

She followed him onto the dance floor going into his arms for a slow country song. They danced together in silence. He had one hand holding hers, and the other was at her waist. He rested his cheek against the top of her head as they slowly swayed to the music, not talking, just enjoying being close.

He was a good dancer, and it was easy to follow his lead. She enjoyed being held by him. He held her just right. He wasn't trying to hold her so close that it felt like he was trying to force her to have vertical sex with him, but he wasn't holding her at arm's length either.

After the song ended, they returned to the table. The waiter had brought their salads, and they talked softly while eating.

Rose had seldom been with a man that she felt this comfortable around. There was a definite attraction, but he was so laid-back, that it was easy to just be in his presence and talk about anything and everything.

She learned that he was thirty to her twenty four. He enjoyed putting on work clothes and helping out with the construction side of things on the job at times. He went to his sister's house every Sunday evening for dinner.

He liked his brother-in-law and enjoyed spending time with his nephew. After they'd finished their meal, they shared a piece of cheesecake with raspberry sauce. She enjoyed the intimacy of sharing a dessert with him. He fed her the last bite, because his Southern manners wouldn't allow him to eat the last one himself. They danced to a couple more songs, before they headed back out to his truck to make the twenty minute drive back to the north part of Arlington.

"What did you think of my favorite restaurant," he asked once they were back on the highway headed south.

"I loved it. The atmosphere was perfect. We were able to talk without yelling, but it was still a fun place. I don't think you could have picked a better place," she told him.

"What did you think of your steak?"

"It was fabulous. It was perfectly tender, and they actually cooked it right. I give it two thumbs up."

He grinned. "I'm glad you liked it. We'll have to go back there sometime. Assuming that you agree to go out with me again," he said.

"You haven't done anything that would make me say no yet," she replied.

"I like that 'yet' like you're waiting for me to do something really stupid," he said.

"I thought you would," she laughed. "So far, no man has disappointed that yet."

"What big plans do you have for tomorrow?" he asked.

"Oh, probably finishing the novel I'm reading. I might go nuts and get my grocery shopping done for the week," she said.

"How would you feel about taking a nice long walk up at River Legacy Park?" he asked.

"That sounds like fun. I could go for that," she said, secretly pleased that he wanted to see her again so soon.

When he pulled up in front of her apartment, he got out and opened her door, holding his hand out for her key. She set the key in his hand, and he unlocked her door for her. "Do you want to come in for a drink?" she asked.

"I'd love to," he responded, following her into the apartment.

She got him some tea from her fridge and grabbed herself a glass of water.

She sat next to him on the couch, and they talked a while. He told her some funny stories about some of the guys at work, and she talked about some of the crazy investors that she talked to on a daily basis. Many of them treated her as if she needed to worship at their feet because of the money they had with her company. She was glad the investors couldn't see her face as they spoke.

After about thirty minutes, he stood up. "It's getting late. I should get home. I'll be back around noon tomorrow to pick you up, if that's all right."

"Noon is fine," she told him. "Do you want me to pack us a picnic lunch? We could find a good spot to stop and eat during our walk."

"I'd like that," he said. She walked him to the door, and he leaned down and gave her a quick peck on the cheek. "I'll see you at noon."

"Good night," she said, as she closed the door softly. She leaned back against it and let out a breath. She had never had a date like that. He had been absolutely polite and hadn't tried anything. She wasn't sure if she was glad that he respected her, or disappointed that he hadn't at least tried to kiss her. She could fall for Alex if given half a chance.

Chapter 3

Rose packed a picnic lunch of sandwiches and some individual bags of chips along with some cookies she baked that morning. She included several bottles of water, and packed it all into a backpack that they could carry along on their walk. The knock on her door came at exactly noon, and she opened the door to find him standing there.

She handed him the backpack with their lunch in it and grabbed her jacket. She would probably only need it for the first few minutes of their walk, but she could always tie it around her waist if she got too hot.

After they were settled into his truck, he asked what she'd fixed for lunch. "Nothing exciting," she answered. "Just some turkey and pimento cheese sandwiches and some chips. Chocolate chip cookies for dessert." She was missing something. She knew she was. "Oh! And some bottles of water in case we get thirsty."

"Did you make the cookies?" he asked.

"Actually I did," she told him. "Don't ever expect it again, though. I only bake when I feel like it. I felt like it this morning."

"I expect nothing from you," he said. "I just enjoy your company. If you hadn't wanted to fix a lunch, I'd have run through a fast food place for us."

She grinned. "You're starting to get to know me already, aren't you? I'm nothing if not unpredictable."

He laughed. "Well, you were there when you said you'd be there, so that was predictable."

"I can stand you up next time to prove my point, if you'd like," she offered with a smile.

"That's okay. I'd prefer to not be stood up," he said.

He held her hand as they walked through the park. The path they walked on was tree-lined and paved. They had both walked it multiple times over years of living in Arlington. As they walked, they talked about the things they saw along the way.

Finally, they reached the end of the path overlooking the Trinity River. It was a nice day for March, and they'd run into a lot of other people along the way. It had been a wet winter, so there was actually a decent amount of water in the river. It would be dried up by the end of summer if they had a normal summer.

"Do you want to eat here, or find a spot off in the woods on the way back," he asked. The area they were in had some concrete benches that would be fine for eating, but there were some areas off in the woods that were similar, but more private, on the way back.

"Let's find a spot in the woods if you don't mind," she responded. "I like the feeling of seclusion in the middle of the city."

"Okay," he grabbed her hand again as they turned and headed back.

A few minutes later, they found a trail off the main path and followed it to a concrete bench. "Is this good?" she asked.

"Perfect," he told her.

They sat down, and he handed her the backpack. She divided up the food between them, and they sat in silence while they ate and drank, enjoying the sounds of nature around them.

When they were finished, they packed all of their trash into her backpack, and she started to stand. He caught her hand and pulled her back down onto the bench beside him and turned toward her. "Is it okay if I kiss you?" he asked. He'd never asked a girl that question before. He'd always assumed it was okay and just done it, but Rose was different.

Rose nodded slowly. She had only been kissed a couple of times. Her philosophy on sex before marriage prevented most men from trying. She turned toward him on the bench. He put his hands on her shoulders and slowly drew her closer to him. He lowered his head to hers for a soft gentle kiss. Their lips barely touched before he lifted his head.

Her eyes were half closed. He looked down at her, waiting for any sign that she didn't like his kiss then lowered his head again. His tongue traced along her lips, and she opened her mouth to him. Wrapping her arms around his neck, she met his tongue with hers.

Rose had never felt this way from a kiss. The warmth spread through her stomach causing tingling throughout her entire body. She ran her tongue along the inside of his upper lip and heard him groan.

Alex lifted his head and lightly pushed her away from him. "You are going to be the death of me," he said.

She sat quietly watching him and wondering why he'd pulled away. Her breathing was deeper than usual, and she could feel her heart pounding. Her lips were still moist from their kiss, and she touched her tongue to her lip to see if his taste was still there.

Alex watched her tongue and felt his groin tighten. They needed to get back to where people could see them. He needed to stop touching her.

He took her hand and led her back to the main path. Just kissing her made him feel so much more than he'd ever felt from sex with other women. She was dangerous.

Rose wasn't sure what she'd done wrong, but she followed along with him. She didn't say anything as they walked. She knew that she didn't have much experience kissing, but could she really have been that bad at it?

When they reached his truck, he opened the door for her and headed back toward her apartment. He drove in silence.

Rose took a deep breath, "I'm sorry."

Alex looked at her in surprise. "What are you sorry for?"

"For making you mad? For being a bad kisser? I don't know. For whatever freaked you out back there," she said in a low voice.

Alex felt like kicking himself. "I'm the one who should apologize, Rose. When I kissed you, I felt like someone had punched me in the gut. Kissing you is sexier than getting naked with most girls. I felt like I needed to get you somewhere public where I couldn't try and take advantage of the situation. I understand now why girls always had to have chaperons until recently."

Her eyes widened. "I see. Can I just say that kissing you turned me on a whole lot too? I've only been kissed a couple of times, but you were definitely the only one who has made me want more than a quick kiss."

"That doesn't help. I love it that you're so blatantly honest about everything, but I could have done without that this time. This is only the second time I've been out with you, and you're already getting under my skin." He shook his head. He'd known he liked her that first night, but what he was feeling now was out of his realm of experience.

"I understand," she said. It was no big deal. They had made no commitments to each other, right? Why did she feel like she was losing so much then? "It's been a fun weekend. Thanks for that."

"I've enjoyed the weekend too. More than I can express," he told her. He needed some time alone to think right now. He wasn't going to be able to go through a long dating process with her. She turned him on too much.

He needed to regroup.

He pulled up in front of her apartment and opened her door for her. Instead of following her inside, he kissed her cheek.

She smiled up at him. "Goodbye, Alex."

"Lock the door after me," he said as he turned to go.

Rose walked into her apartment and sank onto the couch, letting her tears fall. How could she have fallen for him in one weekend? How could she have believed that he might actually want a relationship? She knew better. She always had.

Sensible virginal Rose didn't fall in love in less than 48 hours. She just didn't. She wondered how many times she'd have to tell herself that before she started to believe that she hadn't already fallen in love with him.

*****

Rose got up and worked out before work the following morning like she always did. She pushed herself harder than ever, trying to block Alex from her mind.

At her desk that day, she felt out of it. She answered calls and did her job, but her mind and heart were not in it. She felt like she was working through a thick fog that she just didn't want to find her way out of.

At lunch, her cube-mate, Alicia, cornered her in the kitchen. "What's with you? You're acting weird."

Rose looked up at her. "I'm sorry. I guess I'm just distracted." She wasn't sure she was ready to talk about Alex with anyone. Alicia was her closest friend, so if she could talk to anyone it would be her.

Alicia looked at her with concern for a moment, and then her whole face lit up. "You met a guy, didn't you?"

Rose laughed. "You know me. As soon as I tell them I'm planning on staying a virgin 'til the wedding night, they take off running." Rose tried to make it sound like nothing had happened.

"Who was the guy who didn't? You actually went out with someone didn't you? Come on, Rose, it's me you're talking to. Tell me everything!" Alicia was like a dog with a bone. She wasn't giving up until she got to the meat of the matter.

Rose sighed. "I did meet someone, and I told him what I tell everyone else. We went out on Saturday night and went for a walk in the park and had a picnic yesterday." And I blew it when he kissed me, she thought.

"That sounds promising! A picnic in the park sounds right up your alley! What's his name? When are you seeing him again?" Alicia was practically bouncing up and down with excitement; her short red curls were swaying with her movements, her brown eyes flashing. "You have to tell me everything!"

"His name is Alex. I'm not seeing him again," Rose said, looking down so that Alicia wouldn't see how hurt she actually was over that.

"Why not? What did you say to him?" Alicia asked with a sigh. She knew that Rose tended to be so outspoken that people shied away from her. The ones who got to know her loved her for who she was, but strangers didn't tend to stick around long.

"Why do you assume I said something? Why do I have to be the villain?" Rose felt defensive, even though she knew it was her fault. Somehow.

"You know you always say stupid stuff. Why else would a guy who was willing to put up with your old fashioned weirdness take off?"

Rose shrugged. "I didn't this time. I swear. We kissed in the park, and he said that I was 'getting under his skin', and he dropped me off at home. That was it."

"No way. You had to have said something." Alicia couldn't believe that he would take off just like that. Not if Rose hadn't gone all Rosish and said something completely crazy.

"I really didn't. I mean, I said a bunch of things, but he seemed to like it all." For once, she'd found someone who'd liked her for who she was. At least she thought she had.

"You really liked him, didn't you?" Alicia asked softly.

"Can you fall in love in a weekend?" Rose asked refusing to let the tears shining in her eyes fall.

"I can. I didn't think you could, but I do it all the time," Alicia told her.

"I said fall in love, not fall in lust."

"Oh, well, I don't know then," Alicia said with a wink. "It's so hard to separate the two! Where did you meet him anyway? You didn't mention a date on Friday."

"I met him Friday night doing laundry." Rose waited for Alicia's disgusted reaction and wasn't disappointed.

"Are you still doing laundry on Friday nights?" Alicia sighed heavily. "What is wrong with you?"

"A lot, I guess," Rose said heading back to her desk. She wasn't in the mood to listen to Alicia complain about her laundry night.

Alicia shook her head, trailing along behind her. "Let me fix you up with someone. I'll give him the no sex spiel, but you could just go out and have a good time and get Allen off the brain." That was always Alicia's fix. Find a new one.

"It's Alex. And no thanks. I let you do that once before and it was a disaster, remember?"

She had one time, and one time only given in to Alicia's demands that she let her set her up. The guy had thought he was God's gift to women, and had been certain that he'd be able to convince Rose to give up her ideas of chastity. When it hadn't worked, he'd gotten ugly and she'd had to call a cab to get home. Alicia's ideas of good guys and her own were far apart.

"Well, would you consider having sex with this Alex guy to keep from losing him?" Alicia asked. Alicia had no problems with having casual sex. She said that as long as she made sure to use protection there was nothing wrong with it.

"I don't want a man that I have to change my values for. If he can't accept who I am, and respect my values, then he's not worth having," Rose told her as she sat down and picked up her headset. But she was tempted. Alex was special, and she didn't want to let him go.

Alicia shook her head at her as she got back to work. Rose felt that Alicia was so busy looking for Mr. Right, that she lost too much of herself in the process. She'd even told Alicia that a time or two. Not that Alicia listened to what she called Rose's antiquated moral values.

Chapter 4

Rose got home later than usual that evening because she was working extra overtime during the busy tax season to get more money into savings. By the time she'd eaten dinner, it was after eight and she was exhausted, having gotten up at five so she could work out before work. She was just settling down for the evening when she heard a knock at her door.

She frowned, wondering who it could be as she walked over and opened it. She looked out the peep hole and saw Alex standing there. Why was he here?

Rose opened the door with a questioning look on her face. "Hi," she said. She really hadn't expected to ever see him again. She didn't think to invite him in and just stood staring at him.

Alex leaned down and kissed her cheek and asked, "May I come in for a minute? I know you weren't expecting me, but I want to talk to you for a bit."

She stepped aside and let him in, closing the door behind her. "I didn't think I'd see you again," she told him.

"What? Why didn't you think you'd see me again?" he asked, bewildered.

He hadn't said he'd be by or call, but he thought she knew he was falling for her. Why wouldn't she think she'd see him?

"When you acted strangely after the park yesterday, I thought you were done with me," she told him honestly.

He sighed. "No, I'm not done with you." He took her hand and led her to the couch. "I'm sorry I acted weird. It's kind of a strange situation. I have really strong feelings for you, but I've only known you for a few days. I kissed you, and my body went nuts. You're all I've been able to think about since I met you."

"Is that good or bad?" she asked.

"That depends. Am I having the same effect on you?" he asked bluntly.

She blushed. "Yes. I enjoy being with you. You make me laugh, but I'm really attracted to you, too."

"Well, then it's not so bad. I don't think." He sighed heavily. "You're confusing me. If you were any other girl, I'd be trying to get you in bed. But you were honest and upfront from the beginning that you're not after sex without marriage. I can understand that, and I'm not going to try to pressure you into sex."

She nodded. "I appreciate that." Where was he going with this? "So why don't we go to Vegas this weekend and get married?" he asked.

She laughed sure he was just making a joke.

"I'm serious." The look on his face told her this was no joke.

"This weekend? You want to get married a week after we met?" she asked. "Are you still just looking for a campaign manager in your quest for world domination?" She had to lighten the moment a little. She couldn't think.

He grinned. "I've known for a while that if I met the right girl, I'd be willing to get married. That's why you saying you wouldn't have sex before marriage didn't bother me. I figured that if we got along, we'd just get married," he said.

"Okay, I can agree with that, but this weekend? That's what's freaking me out here. Are you sure you don't want to get to know one another a little better first? I mean, what if I have some deep dark secret that I'm hiding from you?"

"You're too honest and blunt for that. I don't have any either, so what's your next objection?" he asked.

"Well, how do you know we'll get along? I mean, we can obviously be friends, but how do we know that more than that will work for us? We've only kissed once!"

He took the hand he still held in his and pulled her toward him. Leaning down he pressed his lips to hers passionately. He molded her body to his, his hands roaming over her back.

Her hands wrapped around his neck and she returned his kiss for all she was worth. The tingling sensation returned immediately. She felt her heart beat speed up.

Abruptly he lifted his head. "I know. Every time I touch you, I know that you're perfect for me. Marry me."

She looked at him with a confused expression. Fighting to control her breathing, she said, "Can we at least wait a week or two? To make sure we still feel the same way?"

"You're killing me here, Rose. I need you. I don't want to wait that long. I honestly don't want to wait until morning, but I will wait until Friday night. We can fly out and get married that same night." His eyes pleaded with her to say yes.

"You really want to marry me just to have sex with me?" she asked. Was that a good basis for a marriage?

"Right this second, I'd be willing to do anything to have sex with you, but it's more than that. I really think that we're well suited. I don't see any reason to wait," he said. "I haven't had as much fun with a woman in my entire life as I've had with you."

She sat looking at him. She was already half in love with him. Alicia had asked if she was willing to compromise her morals for him, and she wasn't, but was she willing to marry a man she'd known for less than a week?

She pulled his head down for another kiss. She had to be sure that the feelings were as strong as she thought they were. He tasted just as good as she remembered. Touching him made the rest of the world disappear. It was all she could do not to pull him down on top of her right then. She tore her mouth away.

"Where will we live?" she asked. She had to be practical. She had to think. She couldn't let how she felt for him right this second make a decision that would affect every moment of the rest of her life.

"Is that a yes?" His brown eyes stared into hers almost mesmerizing her with the intensity of his gaze.

"I think it is," she answered shyly. She had to take this chance. Maybe it was crazy, but he was offering her a lifetime with the man she loved.

He gave her another hard kiss. "I'll make travel arrangements. What time do you get off work on Friday?"

"I'll cancel my overtime," she said. "I can be home by four thirty."

"We'll plan on flying out at six thirty or later. The wedding chapels are open until midnight, and there's an hour time difference. I think the flight is around two hours. Do you want Elvis to marry us?" he asked.

She laughed. "Absolutely not. If Elvis is there, I'm not getting married!"

"I'll come by tomorrow evening with the specifics of the arrangements," he said, heading for the door. "I'll let you get to bed. I know you have to get up early for work."

She followed him to the door, closing and locking it behind him. She leaned against the door and sighed heavily. What had she just agreed to?

*****

When Rose got to work the next day, she canceled her overtime for the remainder of the week. She wanted to have some time to do some shopping in preparation for her wedding. She wasn't going to wear a long dress with a train, but she did want to have a nice white dress to wear, even if it was simple. She also wanted to pick up some lingerie. For lingerie, she needed a partner in crime.

Alicia was thrilled to go with her after work to shop. The two women headed to the local mall, and Alicia helped her pick out some pretty lingerie.

"I can't believe you're marrying a guy you met last week! It's so unlike you," she told Rose.

Rose grinned. "You haven't seen the guy! Besides, this is the new improved me."

Alicia laughed, holding up a pink night gown. It was a simple cut gown with spaghetti straps that stopped at mid-thigh. It wasn't sexy in a blatant way, but once it was on, it would be fabulous. "This would look so good on you. You've got to get it!"

They had a quick dinner out, and Rose hugged her friend. "Thanks for your help. I'm not much of a shopper, and I've never bought anything that was actually meant to be sexy before."

"No problem. You just have fun Friday night. I want details on Monday," she told her with a grin.

"I promise to have fun. I make no promises about details." She knew she wouldn't be sharing the kind of details that Alicia wanted. Some things were meant to be between husband and wife and no one else.

*****

By the time she got home from work on Friday afternoon, Rose was a bundle of nerves. Alex had said that everything was set for the ceremony. They would take a taxi from the airport to the courthouse and then to the hotel. A limo would pick them up from their hotel to take them to the chapel. After the short ceremony, the limo would take them back to their hotel on the Las Vegas strip.

She had her carryon packed and her dress in a garment bag. They planned to return Sunday afternoon. They'd both taken Monday off work, so they'd have a day to get everything set up like they wanted it. Rose had another month left on her lease, and Alex's lease was up. They decided to combine apartments and would start looking for a home.

When Alex arrived, he gave her a quick peck on the cheek, grabbed her bags and carried them out to a minivan. He'd arranged for his brother-in-law to drive them to the airport and pick them up on Sunday.

As she slid into the van, she noticed the toddler sitting in a car seat in the very back seat. She took the middle seat with Alex. Alex made quick introductions. "This is my kid sister, Sarah the brat, and my brother in law, Clark, and my nephew, Justin." He paused for a moment. "And this is Rose."

Sarah turned around in her seat to get a better look at Rose. "I'm so excited to meet you! I can't believe that you and Alex are getting married. How long have you been seeing each other?" Rose started to respond, but Sarah kept talking without pausing for breath. "Mom is going to hate it that she didn't get to meet you before the wedding, but I'm glad I get to. I'm supposed to call her as soon as I get home and tell her all about you. Where are you guys staying? On the strip? Or in downtown? Do you plan on finding a house in Arlington, or are you looking to move away from here? I'm so glad that I'll finally have a sister. Alex is a big pain, but he's a good brother, so I guess I can put up with him. You need to have a baby right away because Justin needs cousins. It's so fun to have a lot of cousins, don't you think?"

By this time Rose's head was starting to spin. She waited for a moment to see if Sarah was expecting a response. When she didn't say anything else, she said, "A week, the strip, I'm not sure, and yes."

Alex and Clark burst out laughing at the same time. Sarah grinned at Rose. "You kept up with me! I can see we're going to be great friends as well as sisters!"

Sarah was a petite brunette, who looked to be in the advanced stages of pregnancy. "Alex didn't mention you were having a baby!" She glared over at Alex. Why wouldn't he tell her that?

Sarah shook her head and sighed. "Alex is a man. It's not his fault, and we just have to forgive him for his inadequacies."

Rose looked over at Alex and grinned. "So far he seems pretty great to me. Of course, my mother told me at least a hundred times on the phone this week that you never know a man until you've lived with him. She said he's going to leave globs of toothpaste in the bathroom sink, and it will drive me insane. Or he'll be incapable of remembering to take the trash out without being told fifty times."

Sarah laughed. "They're both true in Alex's case! But he's pretty cool anyway. For a brother." She gave Alex a teasing smile.

The van slowed as Clark leaned out the window to get his parking ticket to pay as they left the airport.

"Ignore Sarah. She's just jealous because I got all the brains in the family and she was stuck with the big mouth," Alex said under his breath.

"I heard that! Just for that, I'm not getting you a wedding present," Sarah said.

Clark sighed. "Yes, she is. Don't be difficult, Sarah. We want Rose to think the family is normal. She still has time to back out. Wait to be crazy until after they get back."

Rose laughed at all of them. "I think I'm going to fit in just fine."

Clark pulled up in front of the passenger drop-off, and Alex and Rose got out. Alex went to get their bags. Sarah jumped out of the car as well and hugged Rose. "Best wishes! I'm so glad I have a sister now."

"I've always wanted a sister, too!" Rose hugged her back before walking with Alex into the airport.

After they checked in, and went through security, they only had a few minutes to wait before their flight. "We were cutting it pretty close," Rose commented.

"I know, but the chapel that we're using closes at ten, so we have to hurry," he told her.

"I'm not upset about it. I was just commenting," Rose was extremely nervous around him today. She hadn't been before, but she knew it was the fact that she'd be sleeping with a man she'd only known for a week in a few hours.

Alex could see her nervousness on her face. "I'm glad we're getting married tonight," he told her.

She nodded solemnly. "I am too. I'm just really nervous."

"Are you nervous about the ceremony or about making love for the first time?" he asked her.

"Making love," she responded. "I love being in front of people. I don't know if I'm going to love sex."

"I understand. Don't worry about the sex part, though. It's my job to make sure you love it."

Chapter 5

The two hour flight seemed to fly by. She'd put a book in her purse, just in case, but found that she didn't need it. She and Alex spoke softly as they talked about what they were each looking for in the house that they would soon start looking for.

Rose brought up the possibility of Alex designing their home, and he hesitated. "I'd love to do it, but it would mean a much longer process. We would need to keep renting for another year or two," he said.

"I wouldn't mind that. We could move to a bigger apartment, since we're planning on moving anyway, and then move again when our house was ready. Is that something that you'd really like to do?" she asked.

"I've always wanted to custom design my own home. I really thought that you'd want to be in a home faster than I could put us there by designing it myself, though. And it always felt weird trying to put something together when I knew that someday I'd end up married, and my wife may not have the same taste as I do."

She nodded considering. "I really think that I'd rather live in something that you created just for us, if you don't mind waiting. I'd love to raise our children in a house that I knew you had designed just for our family."

He quirked an eyebrow. "Children? How many are you planning on having? We haven't discussed that."

She shrugged. "I hated being an only child. I don't want any kid to have to feel alone like that. So I'm thinking twenty or thirty would do it," she said.

He coughed. "That may be a few too many for me. How about one?"

She recognized his need for negotiation and got down to it. "How about 20?"

He grinned. "Two."

"Fifteen?"

"Three."

"Ten?"

"Four. And I'm not going any higher than four," he said.

She glared. "Six! That's my final offer!"

"Five, then." He sighed. "What am I going to do with five kids?" Secretly he loved the idea of a big family. A houseful would thrill him.

"Love them," she responded quickly. "And I'll pray the last one is sextuplets and then I get my ten!"

He laughed. "Don't be devious."

She smiled at him. "We haven't discussed birth control. Do you want to start a family right away, or wait a while?"

"Well, if we're having five, we'd better start right away. We need to be young enough to enjoy them," he said with a grin.

"That's what I was thinking!" she snuggled closer to him. They had lifted the arm rest between them for more room, and she found it convenient for being close on the plane as well.

As soon as they landed, they got a taxi and went straight to the courthouse.

The taxi driver took it in stride that a couple would get off the plane and immediately get married. "Happens all the time here," he told them. "Did you bring friends and family, or are you going it alone?"

"It's just us," she said. "We don't want to waste our weekend entertaining when all we really want to do is be alone."

The driver laughed. "I think everyone should get married that way. I wish my wife would have agreed to something like that instead of us starting our marriage thousands in debt for a party."

They got their marriage license, and then headed back to the hotel to change. It felt odd to be changing in the room they were going to be spending the night in, but it wasn't a big deal. She didn't believe that it was bad luck to be seen by the groom before the ceremony anyway.

The ceremony itself was short and to the point. The photographer handed them their CD of wedding photos, and they headed back to the hotel in the limo provided.

In the back of the limo, Alex reached out and pulled Rose toward him, kissing her softly. "So, do you feel married yet?"

She laughed up at him. "Not at all! I think that's going to take a while. Maybe we should take in a show, and go to a casino for a while before we go back to our room. Maybe then I'll feel married." She looked down to hide her grin.

His eyes widened. "Are you serious?" Sighing he said, "I guess we can. I can wait," he said running his hand over her hair. The disappointment in his voice almost had Rose laughing out loud.

"That would make me feel better," she whispered, trying not to shake with laughter. "Let's go back to the room and change, and we'll go out and have some fun. I've never been to Vegas before!"

He dropped his head against the back of the seat. He hadn't thought she was that nervous about making love with him, but if she was then he wasn't going to push it. "What kind of show do you want to see? Magic? Music? Comedy?"

She sucked in her breath to steady her voice, "Oh, definitely comedy. I love to laugh."

Alex noticed that her voice sounded funny, but dismissed it as nerves. The limo pulled up in front of the hotel, and he took her hand, helping her out of the car. After he'd opened the door to their room door, he stepped aside for her to enter. "Why don't you use the bathroom to change, and I'll use the bedroom?" he asked, walking over to his bag to pull out some jeans and a nice shirt.

Rose kept her head down as she took her carryon into the bathroom. She couldn't believe that he actually thought she was going to make him sit through a show or spend time at a casino before she would go to bed with him. She was nervous, yes, but she was more than ready to make love with her new husband. She wouldn't have married him if she hadn't been.

She wasn't one to prolong the feeling of nervousness either. She'd rather bite the bullet and get it over with.

She quickly got ready for bed and changed into the sexy white nightgown she'd bought for her wedding night. It was silky, had spaghetti straps, hugged her curves, and ended at mid-thigh. She couldn't wait to see Alex's face when she walked into the room wearing it. She brushed out her hair so that it fell just right against her shoulders.

Alex changed quickly and sat down on the bed. He was determined to give Rose all the time she needed. He'd rushed her into this marriage, but he wasn't going to rush her into bed with him. Well, he wasn't going to rush her into bed with him right this second. He planned on consummating the marriage that night, but waiting an hour or three wouldn't kill him.

He heard the door open and looked over at Rose with a smile on his face. He didn't want her to think that he was upset with her for asking him to wait for a little while. His eyes widened when he saw what she was wearing.

He immediately stood up and walked toward her, trying not to show his eagerness.

"Please tell me you don't think that's suitable attire for a Las Vegas show," he said quietly as his hands stroked down her arms to grasp her hands in his, pulling her toward the bed.

She laughed out loud. "Only if I'm in the show," she said. The relief in the air was palpable.

He backed toward the bed, holding both of her hands tightly in his. When his legs hit the foot of the bed, she pushed his shoulders and knocked him over onto the bed. She quickly followed him down, pressing her lips to his.

"So you weren't really nervous?" he asked with one eyebrow raised. "Sure, I'm nervous. I'm a lot more excited, though. You, my husband, are hot."

He laughed, and kissed her shoulder. "That sentiment is mutual."

She sat up abruptly. "You're wearing too many clothes," she told him. "I'm sitting here mostly naked, and you're wearing jeans and a shirt. I think you need some help with that." Her hands went to the buttons on the front of his shirt, and she started unbuttoning them quickly.

He laid there watching her with a bemused grin on his face. "Are you in a hurry?"

"I'm in a hurry to get you naked. After that, I think slow would be good!" He sat up so that she could slip his shirt off. "Kick your shoes off." He pulled his socks and shoes off and started to unbutton his pants. She pushed his hands away, and did it for him. "That's my job!"

He laid back and watched as she unzipped his jeans, pushing them down his hips, catching his boxers on the way down. He watched her face carefully as his penis sprang free from his underwear. She pushed the clothes off his feet and knelt beside him, staring intently at his member. She reached out a hand and touched it, stroking it gently.

He caught her hands and flipped her over onto her back. "If you want this to go slowly, then you're not going to be able to do that right now," he told her fiercely, covering her lips with his own. His fingers drifted down to her nipples, and he pinched them lightly through her gown. "I like this thing you're wearing," he whispered. "How offended would you be if I took it off right away?"

She laughed, "I really don't think it's meant to be worn for very long."

He pushed it up over her hips and pulled her to a sitting position, pulling it over her head. "Much better." He pushed her back onto the bed, and immediately brought his mouth to her breast, pulling the nipple between his lips, and laving it with his tongue. The softness of her breast against his face had him groaning, hoping he could hold out long enough to make it good for her.

She arched off the bed, moaning softly. "That feels good." Her fingers threaded through his hair, holding his mouth tightly against her.

His hand roamed across her body to her free nipple, softly plucking the nipple between his fingers and thumb. He kissed his way up her neck and over to her ear, nibbling gently on the lobe. When she shuddered, he smiled. "You're an ear person!"

"Is that good?" she asked.

"Neither good nor bad. I've just never dated one before, but I like ears, so I had to try," he said softly.

"When do I get to kiss you and figure out what you like?" she asked as she laid back and let him nibble at her ear, his hands roaming across her breasts and flat stomach.

He laughed. "Not right now! I'm having a hard enough time waiting as it is. You have to be ready, so just lay back and let me get you there."

"I am ready!" she said.

He shook his head. "Nope. You can speak too coherently to be ready." He moved one hand down to her mound, moving his fingers through the soft hair there. He kissed his way down to her stomach, licking the soft skin around her navel.

He moved his hand down further between her legs. She started to hold her knees tightly together, but then let her legs fall apart. His fingers trailed up her thighs between her legs.

She lay thrashing her head back and forth on the bed. His fingers felt so good.

He moved his hand up slowly to the apex of her thighs, and parted her. His finger found her sensitive nub, and rubbed it insistently. His other hand joined the first and he inserted one finger into her to test her readiness.

She was damp, but not overly so. He slowly began to slide the finger in and out. She moaned softly.

He quickly added another finger, trying to get her used to his touch. Both of his fingers moved in and out steadily faster.

She began to arch against his hand, and that's when he knew she was ready for him. He rolled on top of her, and moved his hips into the junction of her thighs.

He brought his lips back to hers, slowly moving his tongue in and out in imitation of what was about to happen between their bodies. He moved his member to her entrance and pushed softly.

She felt him nudging against her, and was astounded by how good it felt. It was a weird sensation, part pain, and part fullness. He pushed a little harder, and embedded himself fully within her. She let out a sharp moan at the pain, and he laid still, waiting for it to pass for her.

Slowly, the tension left her body, and he began to thrust within her. The thrusts came faster and faster. She started to move with the thrusts, enjoying the sensation now that the initial pain had passed. Slowly she felt her body tightening and grasping for something.

He was getting close. He bit his lip trying to hold out until she finished. He could see in her eyes that she was almost there. A few more thrusts and she closed her eyes and let out a half scream. Thank God. Now he could finish. He moved faster and let out a growl, his body tightening as he poured his seed into her.

He lay there for a minute as his pulse returned to normal. He propped himself up on his elbows to take some of his weight from her, watching her as her eyes cleared and focused again. He dropped a quick kiss to her lips and rolled to her side.

She followed him and burrowed into him, so tired she could only think of sleep. "I liked that. We should do more of it when we wake up," she said against his skin, as she closed her eyes.

He smiled and pulled the cover over her body so she wouldn't get cold. His little virgin bride had more than surpassed his expectations. He couldn't wait to see where the next few days would lead.

*****

Rose woke to strange sensations the following morning. Something was tickling her nipple so she slapped it away. There was a hand on her stomach. That wasn't right. Slowly she opened her eyes. "Oh. Good morning."

He laughed. "Couldn't figure out who was touching you for a minute there, could you?" The humor on his face had her laughing at herself.

"I'm not used to sleeping with anyone. I couldn't figure out what that was," she told him. "I thought it was a bug or something."

"Just your husband trying to get you to hurry and wake up," he said kissing her.

"Why? We're not in any hurry today," she said. "We have all day."

"You may not be, but I am," he answered as he rolled fully on top of her. He began kissing her passionately, his hands kneading her breasts.

"Ahh...I understand now. Your needs were more important than my sleep," she said.

"So glad you see it my way, now be quiet, wife. I'm trying to make love here." He found her propensity for chatting during sex highly amusing.

She seemed to think it was fine to just have a conversation. It was cute. She laughed. "You're doing a lovely job of it, whether I talk or not."

He got back down to business, kissing her neck and ears. "I'll do better if I'm not trying to have a conversation," he said.

"You knew I was a talker before you married me. Did you really think that would change while we made love?" She rolled her eyes at him.

He sighed heavily. "I guess not." He moved a finger inside her to see if she was ready. When he felt her dampness, he positioned himself between her thighs. "Do you think this will make you be quiet?" he asked as he thrust inside her.

She gasped with pleasure. "Probably not," she said, "but I really appreciate the effort."

Chapter 6

Alex and Rose spent the weekend getting to know one another better, both in bed and out. They spent a couple of hours in the hotel casino, and even took in one of the shows. By the time they got back on the plane to return to Texas, she was feeling very secure in her decision to marry Alex.

Maybe he didn't love her yet, but she felt like in time that could happen. She was not looking forward to getting back to the real world. She knew they had a lot of work ahead of them, combining households and then moving as soon as possible. They'd both given notice to the apartment complex the previous week.

The ride home from the airport with Sarah and her family was just as crazy as the ride there. As soon as Alex and Rose got settled into the mini-van, Sarah spun around and asked Rose, "So how was the honeymoon? Is my brother any good in bed?" She had an impish grin on her face.

Rose sputtered and turned three shades of red. Alex threw back his head and roared with laughter. "I didn't think anything would make you blush!"

Rose turned on Alex. "You do realize that your sister just asked me if you were any good in bed right? That's just plain weird, and since I've been in bed with you for the past thirty-six hours, it's blush-worthy, so just get over it! I have to say that I do understand why you call her Sarah the brat now."

Sarah grinned at Rose with wide eyes. "You spent the entire time in bed? You didn't even take in a show?" Sarah had a sister now, and was thrilled to have someone to tease like Alex had always teased her.

Rose groaned. "We took some breaks to eat, watch a show, and we even gambled for an hour or two. We just spent most of the time in bed." She glared at Alex for laughing. "How far along are you?"

Sarah giggled softly. "Nice subject change, sis. I like the way you think!" She didn't answer, but patted her huge stomach.

Rose poked Clark in the shoulder.

"Ouch," Clark said. "No poking the driver."

"Then make your wife and brother-in-law behave please," she politely suggested.

Clark sighed heavily. "It's just not possible. I really think it's some sort of genetic defect."

Sarah slapped Clark's arm. "Genetic defect? What's wrong with you?"

Clark snapped, "Still driving! Don't hit or poke the driver please!" Clark seemed exasperated with the whole lot of them.

Alex was laughing harder and harder. "Sarah, I don't think your brother is getting any tonight. He has a bad attitude," Rose told her.

Clark pulled up in front of Rose's apartment. He turned to look at Rose. "It's not going to work, you know. It won't improve his behavior one little bit. Don't deprive yourself just because you're trying to get him to be good."

Sarah said, "She'd only be depriving herself if Alex is good in bed. Would you be depriving yourself by holding out, Rose?"

Rose opened the door of the van. "I'm done with this conversation. I really am."

"Will ya'll come over for dinner tomorrow night?" Sarah asked. "We usually have Alex over on Sundays, but with just returning from your honeymoon and all, we can forgive you for missing tonight."

Alex looked at Rose. "Let's wait until next week. We have a lot of organization to do to combine households." No one was fooled by that. It was obvious that he wanted to get Rose back in bed and keep her there for a week.

Sarah rolled her eyes at Alex. "Yeah, right. You just want to keep Rose to yourself for as long as possible."

"Of course, I do! I married her because I wanted to spend time with her in bed and out. I got stuck with you." Alex hugged Sarah and carried their bags to the door of Rose's apartment.

He unlocked the door with the key that Rose had given him and carried their things inside. She picked up the bags and began to unpack them when she was stopped by his hand on her arm. "I'm sorry my sister was so annoying."

Rose shrugged. "She's definitely a sister. She's fine. I was just a little embarrassed. I mean, we just got back from our honeymoon, and I know that everyone knows that we had lots of sex, but I didn't need her talking about it!"

He grabbed her hand and started to pull her toward the bedroom. "Do you know how long it's been since I made love to you?"

She glanced at her watch. "Oh, no! It's been over five hours! We're starting to act like an old married couple. Quick take your clothes off and hop on the bed!"

He shook his head at her. "You're being sarcastic. I'm being serious. All I could think about on the plane ride home was making love to you. I was sure that Sarah was going to notice how hard I was in the car and comment on it."

She grinned. "I noticed, but I didn't say anything. I sure hope your sister wasn't staring at you there!"

He unbuttoned her blouse and dropped it on the floor. "You're the only one who can't keep her eyes off me."

She pulled his head down for a passionate kiss. "That's probably a good thing!"

*****

They went to the apartment office first thing on Monday morning. They looked at the two bedroom apartments at the same complex and decided they'd be happy there for the time it took to build their house. They rented one that would be available on Saturday morning. That would make things easier for them with a shorter move. The new apartment was right between their old ones, so would work out well for both of them.

They decided to turn the extra bedroom into an office. One bonus that the two bedrooms had over the one bedroom was a washer dryer was included. No more Friday nights at the laundromat.

They picked up some boxes, and both threw themselves into packing. They both had to work Tuesday through Friday, so having most everything done today would be a help.

Alex got several of his employees to agree to help with the actual move on Saturday.

That night they made sweet love. Rose wasn't looking forward to being away from Alex for the first time since their wedding on Tuesday, but knew that they'd have to go back to the real world.

Tuesday morning Rose fixed breakfast for the two of them. She usually just had cereal, but now that there were two of them, she cooked pancakes. She ran out the door to make it in time to work out before work.

She was glad that Alex was an early riser as well, because she needed to be out of the apartment by 6:00.

When she got to work, she saw a huge "Congratulations!" banner strung across her cubicle. There were balloons tied to her chair. Alicia popped her head up as she sat down in her decorated cube.

"Do you like it?" Alicia asked. She was looking at her speculatively.

"Yeah! Was this your doing?"

"Not the cube! Sex! Do you like sex?"

Rose just laughed. "I told you no details would be given!" She had known Alicia would be asking, though.

"Was it hard to come back to work this morning?" Alicia asked.

"Very." It had been the hardest thing she'd done in a long time.

"Then you do like it! Let me see your ring!"

Rose held her hand out to show off her ring. "I think he did good."

Alicia nodded. "It's beautiful." It was a simple band with three small diamonds. "We're having a party for you this afternoon."

"During tax season? You're kidding!"

"Nope. I talked Colleen into it. She may be a dragon, but she's a romantic. She loved the story of you guys meeting and getting married a week later. So do I for that matter," Alicia responded.

"How was your weekend?" Rose asked, trying to get the conversation off of herself.

"It was great! I met this guy. I decided to do laundry on Friday night to see what would happen. I mean it did work for you! I met no one. So Saturday night, I went to this great nightclub. I met this great guy. He rocked my whole world. And my bed."

Rose rolled her eyes as usual, but for once she understood the appeal of sex. Well, she understood the appeal of sex with someone you love. She couldn't imagine being so intimate with a stranger.

She slipped her headset on and signed into her phone ready for her day. By the time six rolled around, Rose was exhausted. It wasn't just that she was working a lot of overtime. She always worked as much as she could get. Now she was getting a lot less sleep. It would all be worth it, though.

They ordered a pizza and took a packing break to eat after eight. She usually was in bed by nine because of her early mornings, but that wasn't going to happen anytime soon. She yawned as she finished packing up her bedroom. They'd be moving over to pack up his place tomorrow night.

He kept telling her that hers was easier to pack because it was cleaner, but she hadn't been in his yet for comparison.

They finished packing up everything but a last few essentials before heading to bed after eleven. She was so tired she couldn't see straight and fell asleep as soon as her head hit the pillow.

He came in from the shower and looked down at her. He sighed. There was no way he could wake her up to make love to her. He'd have to let her sleep. He would love to wake her, but she was working so hard trying to get them moved in together.

Stripping, he climbed into bed and pulled her into his arms kissing her cheek. If he couldn't make love with her, he could hold her while they both slept.

Chapter 7

The following day, Rose cancelled her overtime for the remainder of the week. She needed to get off work at four if they were going to get his apartment finished before Saturday unless he was greatly exaggerating the mess they were facing.

He picked up dinner on the way home and they ate, and then headed to his place. She steeled herself for the mess she feared was waiting. She wasn't a neat freak, but she didn't tend to like huge disgusting messes and that's what she feared she was facing.

After he'd opened the door, she was stunned to see just how bad the mess was inside. Sarah was right. He was a slob! He'd been good about keeping things picked up after himself at her place, but maybe he was just trying to keep from offending her. Would she still have married him if she'd seen this first? Yeah, she would have. But she'd have grumbled a bit.

He had the same floor plan she had, but his apartment was flipped from hers.

She sighed heavily. "Garbage bags?"

He grinned at her. "Under the kitchen counter. I told you I was a typical male."

"This is worse than typical. This is pathetic!" She shook her head and headed into the kitchen. "Do you want me to start in the kitchen or the bedroom?"

"The bedroom doesn't have as much trash, so you start there. I'll work out here," he answered dropping a kiss on her cheek.

She walked into the bedroom and looked around. The sheet was at the foot of the bed. The blankets thrown on the floor. There was dirty laundry everywhere. She turned around to look at him as he followed her. "What?"

"I've never made love to you on my bed. I thought maybe we could take a little break."

She laughed. "We haven't even started yet! I can't make love on a bed with no sheets!"

He walked to the closet and pulled out a sheet. "I can make the bed."

"You're crazy! This place is going to take a solid month to clean and that's only if we can put our hands on a bulldozer!"

He ignored her as he put the sheet on the bed. He grabbed her hand and tugged her toward it.

"Alex!"

"I didn't get to make love to you last night. It's been over 36 hours," he said. He pushed her down on the bed and followed her quickly, kissing her neck and stroking his hands up and down her body. He slipped his hands under her shirt and rolled her nipples between his fingers through her bra.

She half-heartedly pushed at his shoulders wanting to get everything done, but wanting desperately to make love with him. Lust won out. She gripped his shoulders and tilted her head to the side to give him better access to her neck.

After that, she lost the ability to think. By the time she recovered, she was lying naked beside him with her head resting on his shoulder, both of them breathing hard, and feeling extremely content. She lay there for a minute and finally sat up.

"We've got to get to work. Stop distracting me!" She stood up and pulled on her sweat pants and t-shirt, skipping the bra and panties.

She taped up the bottom of a box, grabbed a big black trash bag, and went into his closet to start packing.

He stayed on the bed for a minute longer and then got up. He pulled on his jeans and went into the kitchen and started clearing away the trash.

Rose had her hair pulled back into a ponytail as she worked. She was amazed at the amount of stuff he had crammed into his closet. She sorted through his clothes as she went and threw away everything that was too stained or torn to wear. It looked like he'd just taken to piling clothes that were no longer wearable in a corner of the closet.

She finished the shelves in the closet and moved on to the nightstand. She raised an eyebrow as she found an unopened box of condoms. She'd known he wasn't a total innocent, but was surprised to find them in his drawer.

At the bottom of the drawer, she found a photograph lying face down. She stared at the picture. It was a woman. She had red hair and laughing brown eyes. She was probably in her mid-twenties. Based on the clothes she was wearing, the picture had been taken within the last few years.

She definitely wasn't Sarah. So who was she?

She laid the picture on the bed, and continued packing, deciding she'd ask Alex about the picture later.

She continued plowing through, packing eight boxes in his bedroom, before going out into the kitchen and living area. "I'm done for the night. I just can't do anymore. I need sleep." She looked around the room. She was amazed at how much he'd gotten done in the time they'd been there. All of the trash was picked up. He had packed four boxes himself. "You've gotten a lot done," she told him, impressed.

"We might make it. I'd like to have everything completely moved and the old apartments cleaned out by Sunday evening," he said.

"That would be nice!" she responded. "I found your condoms by the way."

He had the grace to look embarrassed. "Maybe I should have taken the bedroom," he said.

"Maybe you should have! I have a question for you."

"What's that?" he looked wary. What else could she have found?

She walked into the bedroom and he followed. She handed him the photo she'd found. "Who's this?"

He took the picture and stared down at it. "Where did you find it?" He was trying to stall for time. He knew right where she'd found it.

"In your nightstand." She watched his face carefully. He looked sad. "Who is she?"

He shrugged. "Just someone I used to know."

She waited for him to say more, but when he didn't she picked up her bra and panties and balled them up in her hand. "Are you ready to go back?"

She wasn't sure why it hurt so much that he didn't answer her questions. He hadn't lied about how he felt about her. He'd made it clear that getting married was for sexual reasons and sexual reasons only. It still hurt.

He dressed and they walked back to her apartment together. Neither of them said anything. She noticed that he was still clutching the picture that she'd shown him.

When they got back, he got in the shower, and she changed into a sleep shirt and climbed into bed. She couldn't believe that she could feel more alone with him in the next room than she had in all the years she'd been single. She turned her back to the bathroom door, and lay staring at the wall, tears slowly falling.

Alex didn't even look to see if she was awake when he got out of the shower. He just got into bed and turned his back to her.

*****

They finished up the packing Thursday night, and she spent Friday at the laundromat as always. She washed his clothes along with hers, reading while waiting for the loads to wash and dry. He spent the night loading boxes into the back of his truck so that they'd be ready to unpack first thing in the morning.

She hadn't asked about the photo again, and he hadn't brought it up. She had no idea what he'd done with it after they returned to her apartment.

There was a new tension between them. She wasn't sure if it was in her mind, but it certainly didn't seem to be. He wasn't nearly as affectionate as he'd been. He seemed to have retreated to the other side of an invisible wall that she couldn't get behind. Whoever the woman was, Rose knew that she meant a lot to Alex. Why hadn't he married her?

She looked up as he joined her in the laundromat. "Hi."

He smiled absently and walked over to kiss her cheek, hoisting himself up on the counter next to her. "I've got the truck completely loaded. We'll be able to drop it off as soon as we sign the papers on the new apartment in the morning."

She looked up at him, admiring how he looked with his five o clock shadow across his cheek. She missed the emotional closeness they'd had until she asked him about the photo. She leaned into him and rested her cheek against his shoulder. "It's been a long week."

He wrapped his arm around her. "It has. I'm exhausted. We've both been putting in full days at work, and then another full day at home in the evening. I can't wait until everything is unpacked. It's going to feel like we're on vacation."

They hadn't made love since that evening at his apartment. They'd both been busy and exhausted, but she couldn't help but feel that he would have made the effort if it hadn't been for the picture. She just couldn't get it out of her mind.

She got up to check the laundry after the dryers stopped. Everything was dry, so she pulled the items out one by one and folded or put them on hangers. Alex got up and helped her. They each took a basket and carried them back to her apartment. They hung the clothes in her closet, but left the folded clothes in the baskets. They'd just move it that way the following morning.

She changed into her night shirt and climbed between the sheets as he showered. She lay awake reading, waiting for him.

When he stepped into the bedroom wearing a towel wrapped around his lean hips, he saw that she was lying awake. He dropped the towel and climbed between the sheets beside her. She put the book onto her nightstand and turned to him. She reached out a hand tentatively, touching his shoulder, wondering if he'd take that as the invitation she intended it to be.

He brought her hand to his lips and kissed it softly. He pulled her to him and ran his hands over her soft curves. He made love to her sweetly, but something seemed to be missing to her. He touched her and kissed her and loved her, but there was just something different that she couldn't put her fingers on.

For the first time, she didn't fall asleep in his arms after.

Chapter 8

The move went smoothly. They were finished by early afternoon on Saturday, and both apartments were cleaned and keys turned it by late Sunday morning.

Alex and Rose drove to Sarah's house in the south part of Arlington that evening. When they arrived, Alex joined Clark in the living room playing with Justin. Rose wandered into the kitchen to help Sarah with the meal.

She was in the process of peeling a small mountain of potatoes and Rose picked up a knife to help her.

"Why don't you look happy?" Sarah asked.

Rose shrugged. "I'm just tired. We orchestrated a move and packed millions of boxes in a week. Just cleaning Alex's apartment was the work of eight women."

Sarah laughed. "It was awful. I know. Before Justin was born, I used to go over and clean it weekly. After he came along, I just didn't have the time anymore." She cut up a couple of potatoes and plopped them into a huge pot of hot water. "That's not what I meant though. You do look tired, but there's sadness there, too. What's wrong in honeymoon land?"

Rose fought an internal battle. Should she ask Sarah about the picture? Or should she just wait for Alex to tell her what happened? She needed to know. Maybe what she found out wouldn't be a good thing, but anything had to be better than not knowing anything at all.

"When we were packing up Alex's apartment, I found a picture," Rose told her.

The way Rose spoke told Sarah who it was, but still she asked. "Red hair? Brown eyes? Beautiful?"

Rose nodded. "Who is she?"

"Her name was Becky." Sarah looked down as she answered the question. Alex should have told Rose all of this. But he hadn't, and Rose had a right to know.

"Was?" Rose raised an eyebrow.

"She was killed in a car wreck two years ago."

"Was she Alex's girlfriend?" Rose asked.

"She was his fiancé. She died a month before the wedding. She was hit by a drunk driver," Sarah said.

Rose looked down. "He still loves her." Rose had known from the moment that she asked about the photo that he loved the girl in it. He'd have talked about it otherwise.

Sarah shook her head. "He wouldn't have married you if he still loved her. He wouldn't have done that. He spent a long time not able to even smile, but in the past year he's been laughing and joking again. He hadn't mentioned another woman until he came here two weeks ago. He was so distracted. I kept teasing him about being twitterpated. Like in Bambi."

Rose shrugged. "He's been different since I asked him about the picture. It's like he's built a wall between us. What was she like?"

Sarah was silent for a moment while she thought about how to answer that question. "Well, she was beautiful, but you already know that. Alex was wrapped around her little finger." She paused for a moment moving the pot of potatoes onto the stove and turning the burner on high. "Alex had a blind spot where Becky was concerned. She was extremely self-centered. The wedding plans were a nightmare. You know all those TV shows with Bridezillas? They were based on Becky."

Rose's eyes widened. "Are you saying that just to make me feel better?" Why would Alex have fallen for a girl like that?

Sarah shook her head. "Alex would strangle me if he knew I was saying this at all." She turned to look at Rose fully. "She wasn't going to let me be in the wedding until she found out that I was pregnant. When she realized I'd be around six months along for the wedding, then I was in. She came right out and told me that only fat and ugly women could be in the wedding party. They'd make her look better."

"She wasn't kidding? That sounds like something I would have said as a joke." Rose was having a hard time believing Alex could have loved a woman like that. He seemed to be so much more grounded.

"She wasn't kidding. She was a witch with a capital B. Mom and I tried to talk to Alex about her, but he just got angry. She told him that we were mean to her when he wasn't around. Finally, Mom and I started to treat her like a princess just to keep Alex from hating us. It worked, but it drove us nuts. I shouldn't talk badly about her. She's dead. I don't have a nice thing to say about her, though. Well, she was beautiful. I guess that's nice."

Rose was silent through dinner as she thought about what Sarah had said.

As the two women did dishes together after the meal, Rose said, "Please don't tell Alex that I asked about Becky."

Sarah shook her head. "I won't. If I told him that, I'd have to admit to what I said about her." She knew she'd have to talk to him about it again eventually, but she wasn't ready yet.

Rose nodded. "If you were me, how would you proceed? Should I press him with questions about her, or just let it go? He's seemed sad and distant since I showed him the picture."

Sarah sighed. "I wish I knew the answer to that. I think he probably needs time to think about how he wants to talk about it. No matter what she was, he loved her. And Alex doesn't do anything halfway."

*****

Tax season was finally over and Rose was able to cut back her obscene hours at work. They'd been married four weeks, and Rose felt like they were drifting further and further apart. She was sure that Alex felt like he'd made a mistake to rush into marriage with her, but she felt just the opposite. She loved him more every day.

As she started spending more time at home, she realized just how much time he was spending locked away in the home office they'd set up.

Finally, she asked him what he was doing in there.

He looked startled. "I'm planning our house. I thought you knew." He'd worked hard every night to get it just perfect. They'd be ready to look for a home site soon.

"Really? May I see what you've done so far?" she asked tentatively.

"Of course!" He grabbed her hand and pulled her into the office. "Have you ever looked at a blue print?" he asked.

"Not really."

He pointed out the features that would interest her most. "The master bedroom is here. There are two large walk-in closets. I've drawn the bathroom with a separate bath tub and shower. I've drawn a separate alcove for the toilet with its own door so that we don't have to worry about walking in on each other."

She nodded. "That bathroom looks huge!" She loved big bathrooms.

"I thought you'd like that. If you want me to change something, just let me know."

"So far so good. How many bedrooms are there total?"

"Five bedrooms and three baths. I put one bedroom right next to the master. I thought we could use it for a nursery. Then the other bedrooms are across the house for when the kids get older."

"So you're still willing to have five kids?" she asked with a grin. She'd been unsure what he wanted from her for a while.

"Why wouldn't I be?" he asked surprised.

She studied him for a moment wondering if this was the time to bring up how she'd been feeling. "You've just seemed a little distant since we got back from Vegas."

He pulled her down into his lap. "I'm sorry I've seemed that way. I don't mean to be distant." She was his whole world. He didn't want to give any woman the kind of power over him that saying that would, though, so he remained silent.

"I was starting to worry that you regret our marriage," she said softly.

He sighed. "I don't regret our marriage at all. We got married fast, and need to take time to get to know one another a lot better, but I don't regret our marriage. I'm sorry that I made you think that." He hadn't meant to make her feel insecure. He wanted to kick himself for hurting her that way.

She snuggled into him, burying her face into his shoulder. She felt like he knew everything in the world about her, but he'd completely closed off a couple years of his life from her. The years with Becky in them. She didn't want to bring that up now, though. It was too nice to just sit with him and talk about their future.

"We only really had those two days alone together when we went to Vegas. Since we got back, I feel like all we've done is work. How would you feel about taking a long weekend somewhere?" he asked. "I don't feel like we've had the time we need to truly talk. And spend entire days making love of course. We need that."

She smiled. "That sounds nice. Where are you thinking about going?"

"Maybe a cabin on a lake somewhere? I'd rather go in May, before school is out and the family traffic gets in. And before the oppressive Texas heat makes actually being outside not much fun. Unless you'd prefer to go somewhere like Vegas or Branson?"

"No, a lake sounds great. I like the idea of actually having some time alone. Of course, it means I'll have to cook a lot more than I usually do, but I'll live," she grinned. "Maybe we could find a cabin near a nice restaurant?"

"We'll take steaks and I'll grill out some too. That way all the work doesn't have to be you." He liked the idea of doing something for her.

"Set up the time and place, and let me know as soon as possible. This is a good time of year for me to take off work for a couple of days," she said.

"I've been meaning to talk to you about that, too. You know, we don't need the money you make. I can easily support us both and then some. Do you want to start looking around for a location for your book store?" he asked.

Her eyes widened. "We've never really talked about money, but it never occurred to me that would be possible."

He smiled. "If you were to save every dime you made, how long would it take before you could get your store?" He knew how much she hated her job. It seemed to drain everything from her. He wouldn't mind if she wanted to just stay home, but knew that she wasn't the type who could do that without going insane.

She thought about that for a minute, doing some mental calculations. "Probably four or five months?"

"If I could add around $20,000 to your savings? Then how long?" He could add a lot more to it than that, but he knew she had a good chunk already saved.

"Then I could quit tomorrow," she said. "But I don't expect you to do that." She'd never felt like she should live off him. They didn't exactly keep their money separate, but she felt like she should pull her own weight.

"Why not? I can easily do that, and you'd be able to do what you want to do. Would you like to do that right away?" he asked.

She thought about it for a minute. It never occurred to her that he'd help her open her store, but there was no reason to say no. He was her husband, and any money she made would be shared by them. "Absolutely. I'd love to never have to wear an antenna on my head again," she told him.

"Give your two weeks' notice on Monday then. We'll scout around for a location for your store. I'm assuming you want to open it here in Arlington?" he asked.

"I was actually thinking Grand Prairie. Arlington has a couple of used book stores, but there aren't any in Grand Prairie at all. It wouldn't be too far from here, and I think I'd drive more traffic into my store that way. There are a couple of empty shops on 303 that I've been eyeballing for a while, hoping they wouldn't be rented out before I was ready."

"We'll drive over there and take a look tomorrow," he said. "If there's a place worth having, we'll lease it. Do you know anything about keeping books for a business?"

"I've never done it, but I've done a lot of research on it. I have an idea on how I want to run things. With the amount you're pitching in, I'll have enough for operating expenses for the first three months. Hopefully after that, even if I'm not making a lot of money, I can handle the expenses as they come along."

"Hopefully we can find something tomorrow. Do I get to build the bookshelves," he asked with a gleam in his eye. He loved the idea of working with his hands and helping her in the process.

"Well, I was going to buy cheap ones, but sure! I'll take all the help I can get!" She waited a moment. "I'll even see if I can come up with some way to......compensate you for your time."

He grinned. "Do I get compensation for offering?"

She kissed him. "Will that work?"

He stood and led her into the bedroom. "It's certainly a good start!"

*****

They found the site she wanted to use for her bookstore the following day, and she gave notice on Monday morning. She was thrilled. The next few weeks were full of preparations for the book store. They decided to open on June first, which meant a lot of work had to be done in the meantime.

They took the second weekend of May to go to the lake. The relaxation and just plain time away from life was refreshing. They left on Friday morning and the plan was to return on Monday evening. They went to a cabin on Lake Fork about a two and a half hour drive from Arlington.

On Saturday morning, after a good breakfast, Rose finally broached the subject that she hadn't been able to get out of her mind. "I want to talk to you about something, Alex."

He looked up from the book he'd been reading while she showered. "What's that?"

She took a deep breath. "I talked to Sarah about the picture that I found in your night stand. She told me about Becky."

A shuttered look fell over Alex's face. "What about her?"

"I want to know if you're still in love with her. If you are, I don't see how we can make our marriage work," she said honestly. She'd thought long and hard about how she was going to bring this up, and had decided that the direct approach, while more painful at times, was the best approach in this case.

Alex sighed. "No, I'm not still in love with her. She's been dead for two years, and I'd just like her to stay that way."

"Will you tell me about her? Sarah gave me her opinion and her perspective on everything that happened, but I'd love to hear it all from you. You knew her best." Rose knew that now that he was starting to talk about it, she needed to press the subject until they got it all out in the open. He laughed at that. "I thought I knew her best. Sarah and Mom both thought I was nuts to want to marry her. They kept telling me that she was a self-centered witch, but I just didn't see it. Not at first. It just kept making me angrier and angrier that they were so against her."

She frowned. "What happened to make you think they were right?"

He shrugged. "It was never one big thing, more like a lot of little things.

She always acted like my opinions were important to her, but when we made a decision together regarding the wedding she would go behind my back and change it. She wouldn't let Sarah be in the wedding, which I really wanted, but then finally, when she found out that Sarah would be showing a great deal at the time of the wedding, she asked Sarah to be in it. One of her other friends was extremely overweight, and lost over fifty pounds. Becky picked a fight with her and took her out of the wedding party."

Rose looked at him contemplatively. "She sounds interesting." She had known most of this from Sarah, but was glad to hear that he had seen it for what it was.

Alex grinned. "That is a huge understatement." He sat looking down at the paper for a minute. "I thought about breaking it off, but felt like being engaged was a commitment. I didn't want to back out. Then I found out she was sleeping with a friend of mine. Well, a former friend. He came to me and told me he was in love with her and she was afraid to break it off with me. When I confronted her, she admitted it, but said it had all been a mistake. He'd pressured her into bed with him."

Rose shook her head. "I see. Did you believe her?"

"I'd already noticed too many weird things about her story to believe her. I told her that I was done with her. She took off. Three hours later I got a call that she'd been killed in car crash. Hit head on by a drunk driver.

Apparently, she'd left my place, and gone straight to a bar. She was hit on her way home. Her alcohol content was just barely under the legal limit. I don't know if she'd have been able to stop if she hadn't been drinking."

Rose sat thinking for a minute. "Why didn't you tell me about her?"

"Why would I tell you about her? She's been gone from my life for two years. No one knew that we'd broken it off before the wreck, so I played the grieving fiancé. I had no desire to date again for a while. I wanted nothing to do with another woman who could mess with my mind the way she had," he said.

"Sarah thought you were grieving and hadn't been able to see past that to anyone else."

He laughed. "I did grieve for the life I thought I'd have with her. I thought I'd found the perfect woman." He knew he'd found the perfect woman now. Well, perfect for him, anyway.

"I'm sorry you went through that," she said. She walked over to sit beside him on the couch, and stroked his arm.

He turned to her. "I've never told anyone the full truth of what happened between us. I just didn't feel like I wanted to dredge all that up again."

She sat thinking about all he'd said for a minute. "Why did you still have her picture?"

"Every time I met a girl that I thought I wanted to start a relationship with, I'd get out her picture and look at it. It was my way of reminding myself what I didn't want from life. I don't want a Becky in my life." He ran his fingers along her jaw. "I want a Rose in my life. I want someone who will give of herself and truly care about me."

She turned her head and kissed the palm of his hand. "I can't think of anyone I'd rather spend my life with."

He lowered his head and kissed her. "I thought that I was in love with Becky right up until a couple of months ago. And then I met this girl in a laundromat and knew almost immediately what love really feels like. What I felt for Becky was lust. I was in thrall of her beauty. But you, Rose, you turned my world upside down when you helped me sort my laundry and told me that you wouldn't have sex before marriage."

She smiled, her whole face lighting up. "I love you, too. I knew after our first date that I loved you. I wouldn't have married you otherwise."

He pulled her close and hugged her tightly. "I need you in my life. I'm sorry that I made you feel like I was still in love with Becky."

"No need to apologize. I understand why you didn't want to talk about it. Please try not to shut me out about things like that again. I'm confident, but even I'm not that confident." She snuggled into him. "I do have one more thing to talk about."

"What's that?" he asked.

"I saw the doctor Thursday morning. The first of five will be born in about eight months," she grinned. She had wanted all to be right between them before she told him. This seemed the perfect time.

"Seriously? That was fast! Should you be doing all the work you're doing for the book store then? Should we put that off?" he asked.

"I'm doing some interviewing this week for a couple of employees. With help, I'll be able to go to the doctor whenever I need to. All will be good. Of course, you'll have to give up your office, and let me turn it into a nursery," she said with a grin.

"I can handle that. Just so you and the baby are healthy."

Epilogue

Rose looked around the store with a stunned expression on her face. It was packed. She hadn't expected an opening anywhere close to this one.

She'd decided to do have her grand opening on a Saturday, when she would have the most potential for traffic.

Both of her employees were working today and Alex was helping out as well. It was taking all four of them to cover all the customers swarming through her store. She'd decided to specialize in the two genres that she was most familiar with, romance and science fiction. She'd deliberately marketed to those two segments. Obviously it had worked.

She stretched and shifted as she checked out yet another customer. There had been a steady stream of customers buying things since they'd opened the doors a little over six hours before.

Alex saw her, and walked to her side. "You need to take a break. They can handle it for a while. The doctor said you needed to put your feet up for ten minutes every four hours. It's been six." He signaled to one of her new employees to take the register.

She nodded tiredly and headed into the back room. She'd made a small office space with a loveseat so that she could rest when necessary. Alex followed her in.

She smiled up at him. "This is so much more than I ever dreamed it could be." She sat down on the loveseat and rested her feet on a small ottoman.

"Thank you so much for being so supportive. I promise I won't make you come in and work every Saturday."

He sat next to her, pulling her into his side. "On Saturdays that I don't have to work, if you're working, this is where I'll want to be. I want to be with you every minute that I can."

9 798223 054368